Praise for
STORY SPINNERS

"Reading *Story Spinners*, I couldn't stop thinking about my own sister. We're so different sometimes, but in the end that just makes our stories interesting. It's a book for anyone with a sibling who's hard sometimes but well worth the work. In the end it made me feel happy and warm (and want to go call my sister)." **—Dana Simpson, creator of *Phoebe and Her Unicorn* and *Ozy and Millie***

"*Story Spinners* is an ingenious concept masterfully executed. Both kids *and* adults will be captivated by these characters and enthralled by the brilliantly intertwined stories. I just can't say enough great things about this one-of-a-kind, laugh-out-loud graphic novel. Now hurry up and read it!" **—Jarrett Lerner, author and illustrator of *A Work in Progress***

"Classic Cassandra Federman! A clever, fun, and fantastically spun story (within a story!) that caught me in its wonderful web of heart and imagination." **—Ben Clanton, *New York Times* bestselling author and illustrator of the Narwhal and Jelly series**

STORY SPINNERS

ALSO BY
CASSANDRA FEDERMAN

This Is a Sea Cow

This Is a Seahorse

STORY SPINNERS

A Sisterly Tale of Danger, a Princess, and Her Crew of Lady Pirates

Written and illustrated by
CASSANDRA FEDERMAN

ALADDIN
New York London Toronto Sydney New Delhi

This book is a work of fiction. Any references to historical events, real people, or real places are used fictitiously. Other names, characters, places, and events are products of the author's imagination, and any resemblance to actual events or places or persons, living or dead, is entirely coincidental.

ALADDIN
An imprint of Simon & Schuster Children's Publishing Division
1230 Avenue of the Americas, New York, New York 10020
First Aladdin edition March 2025
Copyright © 2025 by Cassandra Federman
All rights reserved, including the right of reproduction in whole or in part in any form.
ALADDIN and related logo are registered trademarks of Simon & Schuster, LLC.
For information about special discounts for bulk purchases, please contact Simon & Schuster Special Sales at 1-866-506-1949 or business@simonandschuster.com.
The Simon & Schuster Speakers Bureau can bring authors to your live event. For more information or to book an event contact the Simon & Schuster Speakers Bureau at 1-866-248-3049 or visit our website at www.simonspeakers.com.
Book designed by Laura Lyn DiSiena
The illustrations for this book were rendered digitally.
Manufactured in China 1124 SCP
10 9 8 7 6 5 4 3 2 1
Library of Congress Cataloging-in-Publication Data
Names: Federman, Cassandra, author, illustrator
Title: Story spinners : a sisterly tale of danger, a princess, and her crew of lady pirates / written and illustrated by Cassandra Federman.
Description: First Aladdin hardcover edition. | New York : Aladdin, 2025. | Audience: Ages 7 to 10. | Summary: Polar-opposite, "forever-fighting" sisters, Kennedy and Devon, come together to tell an epic bedtime story that stops their baby sister's crying, so they can finally all get some sleep.
Identifiers: LCCN 2022000417 (print) | LCCN 2022000418 (ebook) | ISBN 9781665918237 (hardcover) | ISBN 9781665918244 (paperback) | ISBN 9781665918251 (ebook)
Subjects: CYAC: Graphic novels. | Sisters—Fiction. | Storytelling—Fiction. | Cooperativeness—Fiction. | LCGFT: Graphic novels.
Classification: LCC PZ7.7.F43 St 2024 (print) | LCC PZ7.7.F43 (ebook) | DDC 741.5/973—dc23/eng/20220412
LC record available at https://lccn.loc.gov/2022000417
LC ebook record available at https://lccn.loc.gov/2022000418

For my BFF (best-friend-forever), Erin "Skin" Brewster, who introduced me to comics in fifth grade. I miss our Wednesday walks to Wild Time Comics.

Chapter 1
SISTERS

DEVON

pet tarantula
heavy metal
artwork
Doom $kullz
graphic novels
pirate stuffie
unmade bed
messy floor
sports gear

"Naw ihts nhat!"

These FFSs have only three things in common.

Chapter 2
THE OTHER SISTER

And they hate that they can't do this when her crying keeps them up... ALL... NIGHT... LONG.

Thwip *Thwip*

DRONEMASTER

(Fortunately, drones are for ages thirteen and up.)

And because Kennedy and Devon are so *tired* they've gone from FFSs to FTTDSs. (That's "fight-to-the-death sisters.")

DEVON 99 KENNEDY

FIGHT!

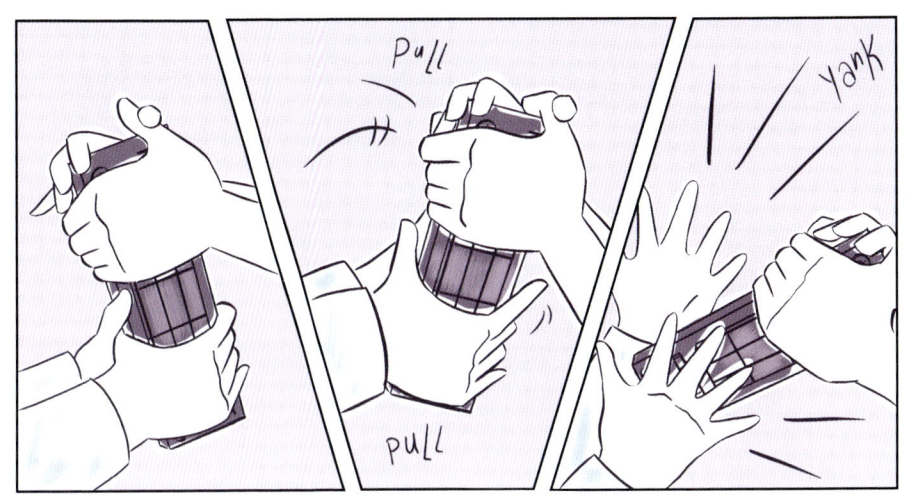

Chapter 3
GETTING ALONG

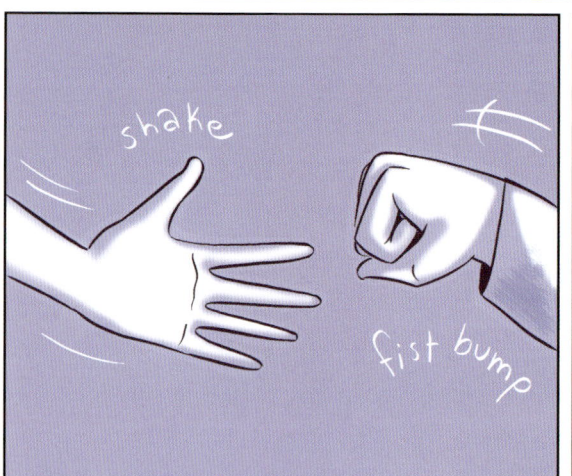

Chapter 4
THE FAIRY TALE... BEGINS?

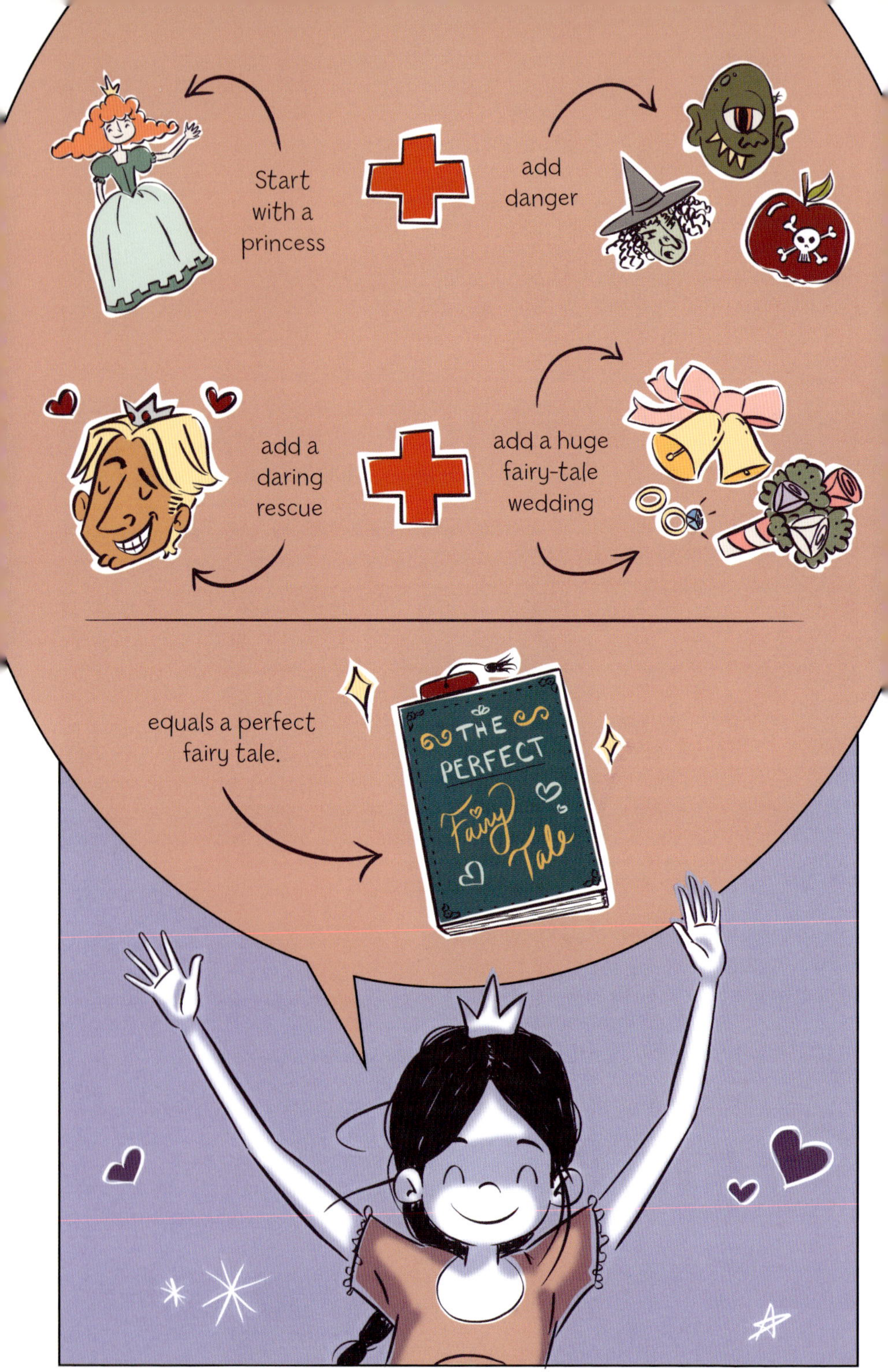

Start with a princess ➕ add danger

add a daring rescue ➕ add a huge fairy-tale wedding

equals a perfect fairy tale.

THE PERFECT Fairy Tale

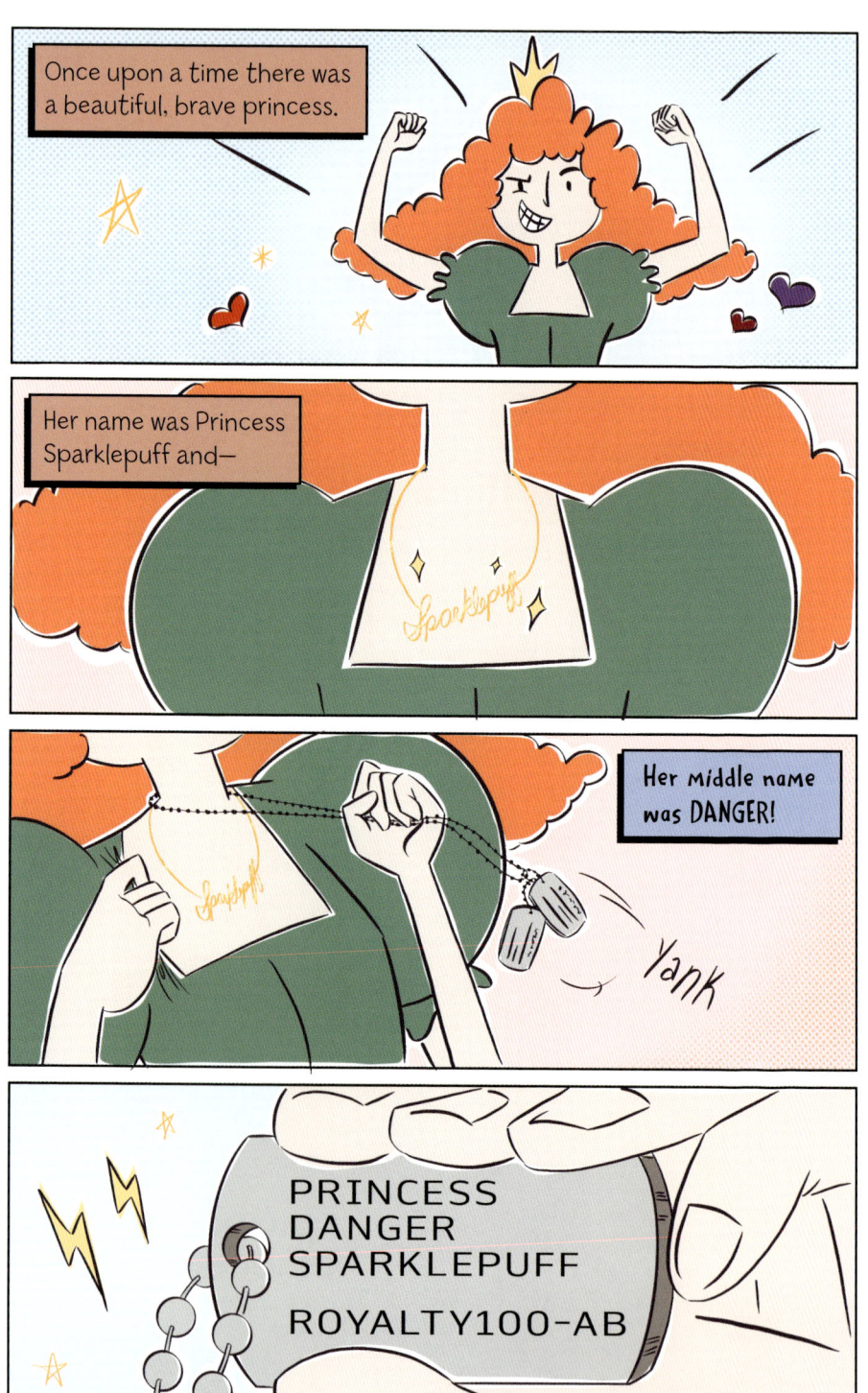

...that Sparklepuff was ever so sad. Because unlike other luckier princesses, she had never been...

...cursed... ...or captured... ...or poisoned.

SLEEPING BEAUTY

RAPUNZEL

SNOW WHITE

WAHHH!

Chapter 5
TAKING DANGERY ACTION

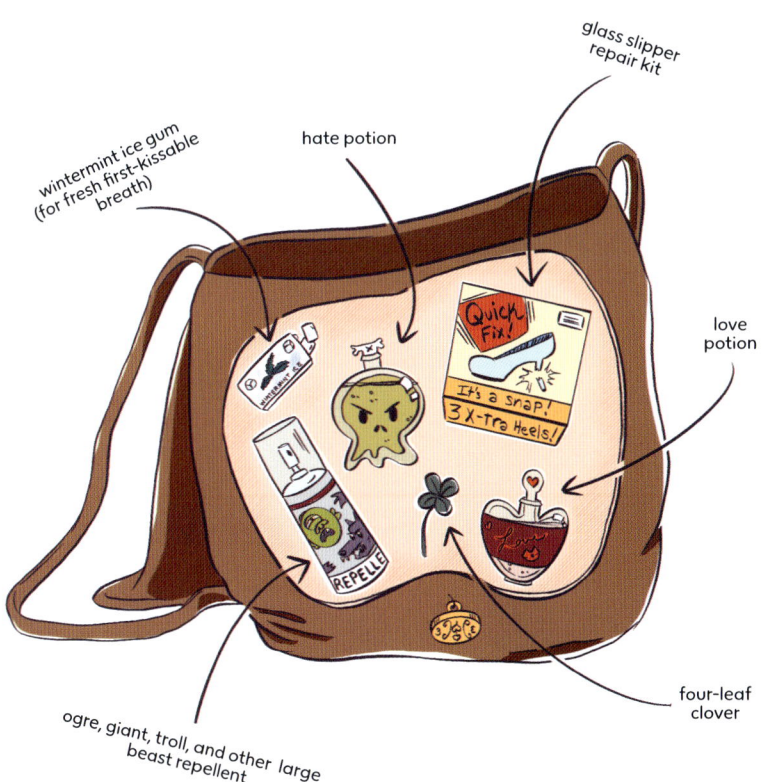

Princess Danger Sparklepuff boarded her ship— with her crew of Lady Pirates cuz pirate ships have pirate crews.

Yo.

Sup?

TOOT!

Then the—ONLY—pirates in this story set sail for the island of—

POOPIES!

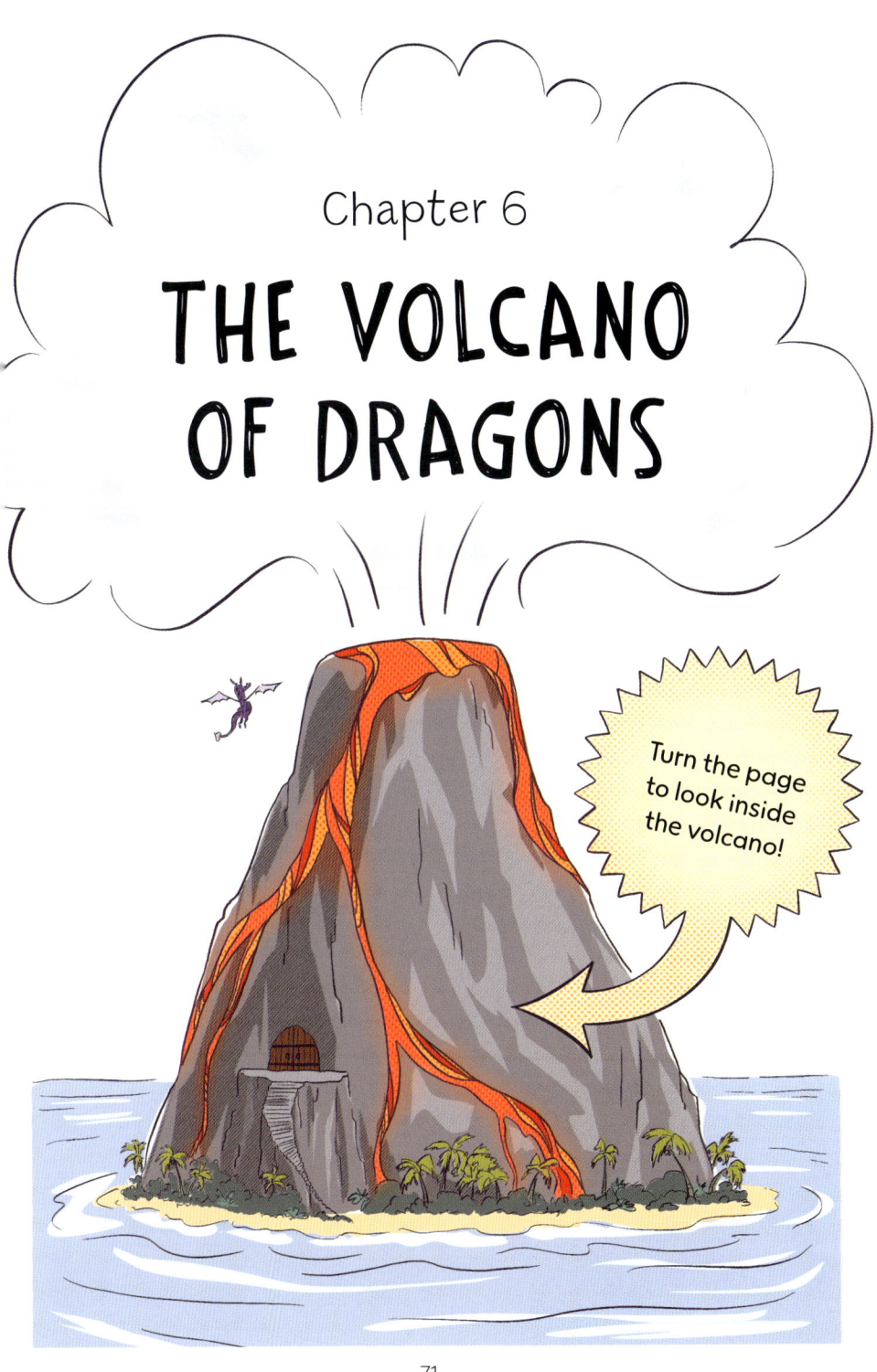

Sparklepuff approached the Dragon King's lair—

And bashed down the door!

BASH!

Greetings, Dragon King.

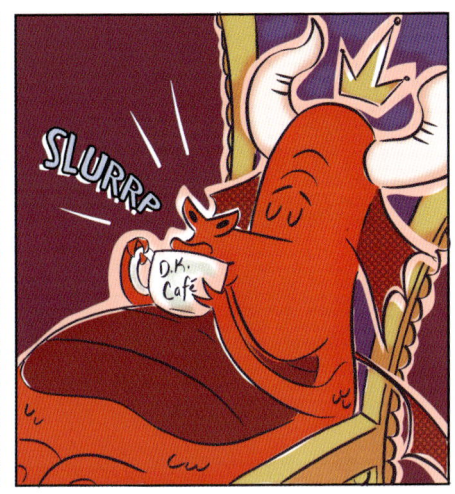

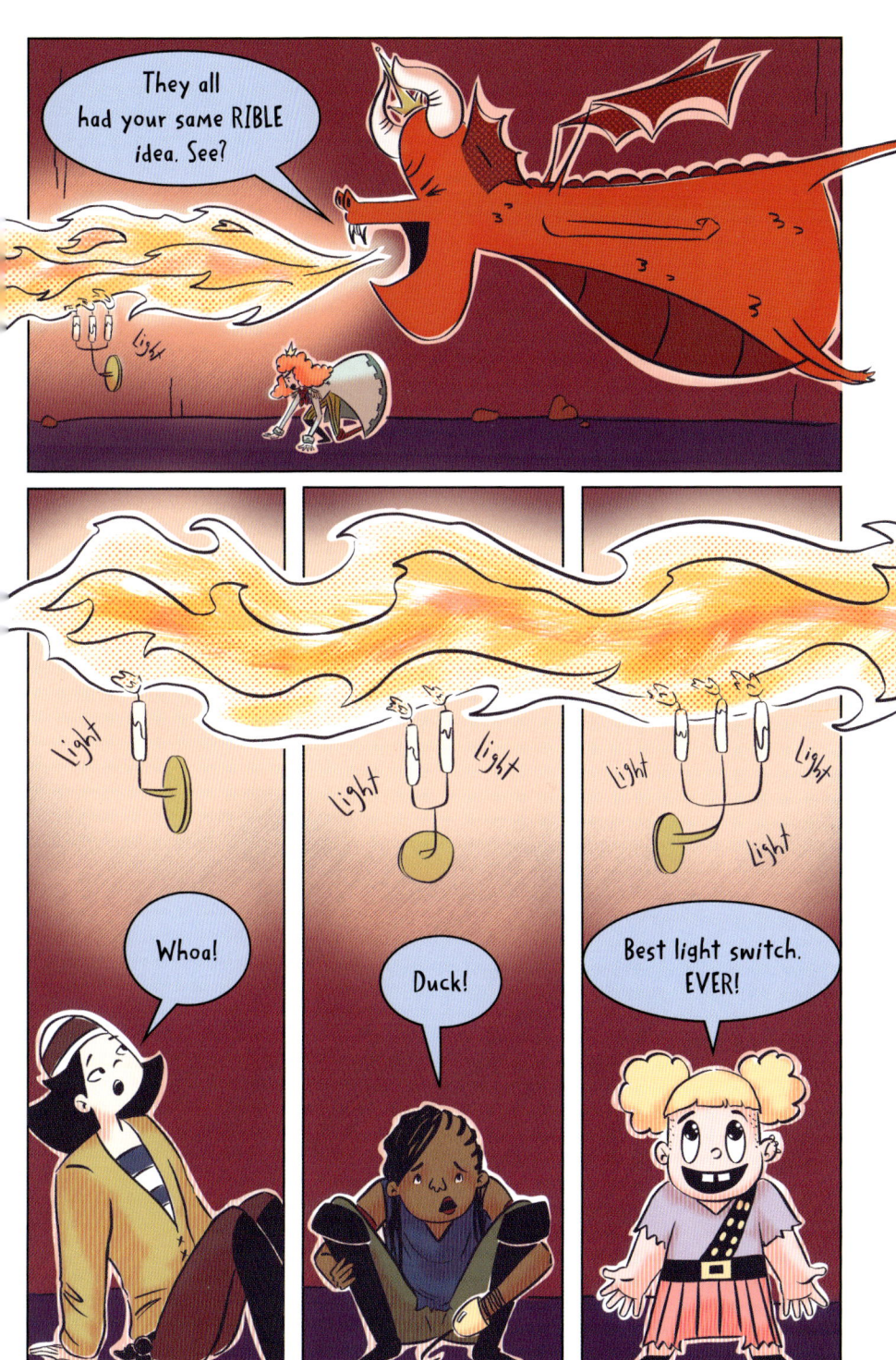

Chapter 7
AXES 4 ALL

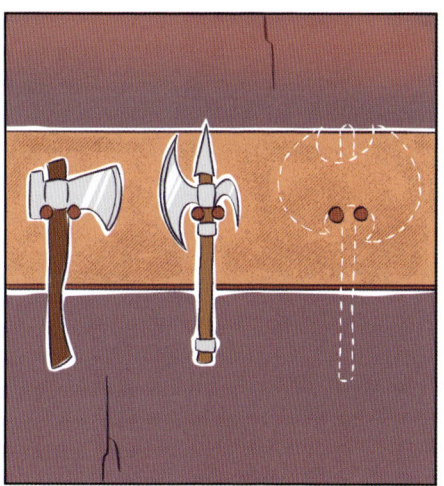

The delicious pizza filled Sparklepuff's belly, but it could never fill her heart. Only TRUE LOVE could do *that*!

BURP!

She could not give up! She would become the Dragon King's prisoner!

Just like *that* princess with the beautiful jewels.

And *that one* with the fanciest dress ever.

Chapter 8

PRINCESS PURPLEBOTTOM'S QUEST

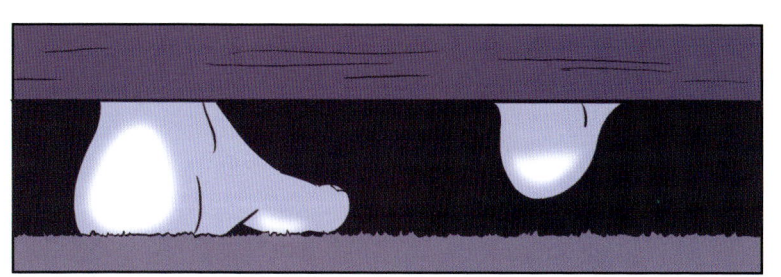

Chapter 9
THE WICKED WATER SPIDERS

"Check out all this free swag we got!"

"I'm nevah gonna wash my abdomen again!"

Stay Stinky! — Emperor Garbage Truck

Chapter 10

GARBAGE KINGDOM

Chapter 11

HOW PRINCESS DANGER SPARKLEPUFF FIXED EVERYTHING

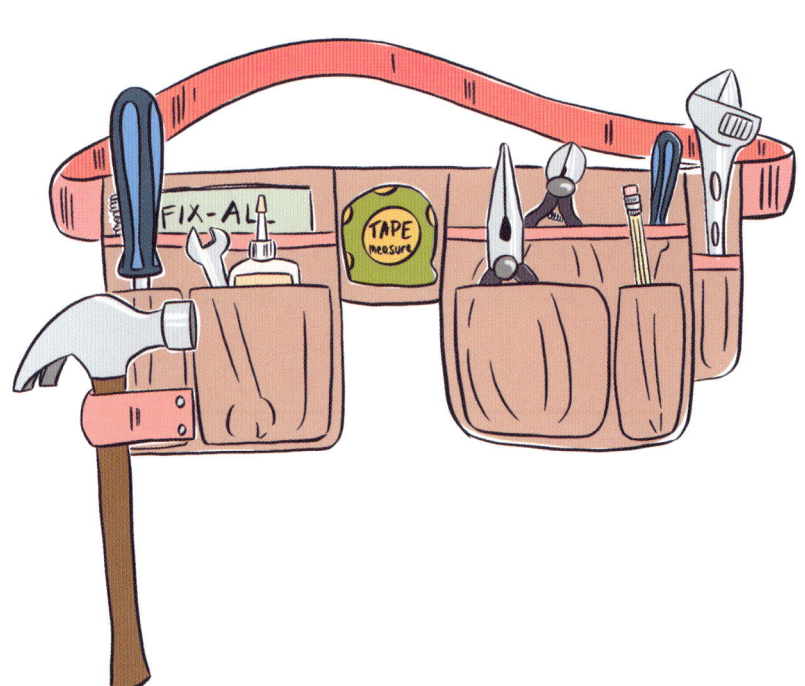

After the Agreement was signed...

Sparklepuff and her crew of Lady Pirates escorted the Shark Prince to...

As Sparklepuff said goodbye to her crew of Lady Pirates, she thought about all the weird creatures they'd met...

She thought about all the problems they'd solved...

And the fun they'd had together...

And she didn't feel excited about meeting her Prince Charming anymore.

Instead she felt rible. She felt so rible that she—

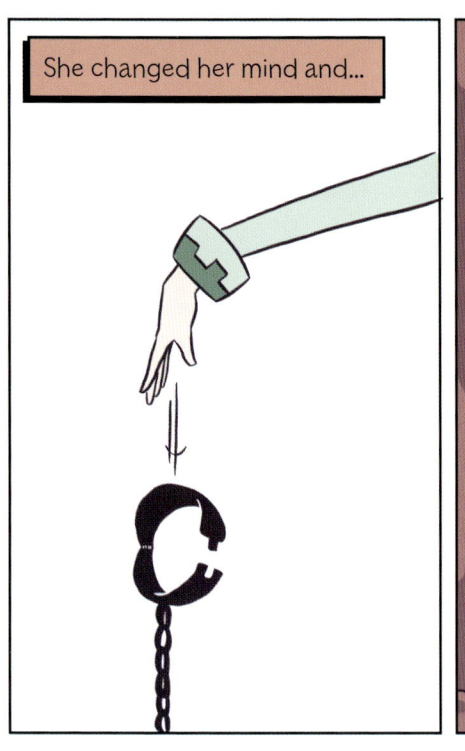

"We did it!"

"Yup! Turns out we tell pretty awesome stories together."

Zzzzzzz

CHAPTER 12

GOOD NIGHT? FOR REAL?

Chapter 13
SISTERS (AGAIN)

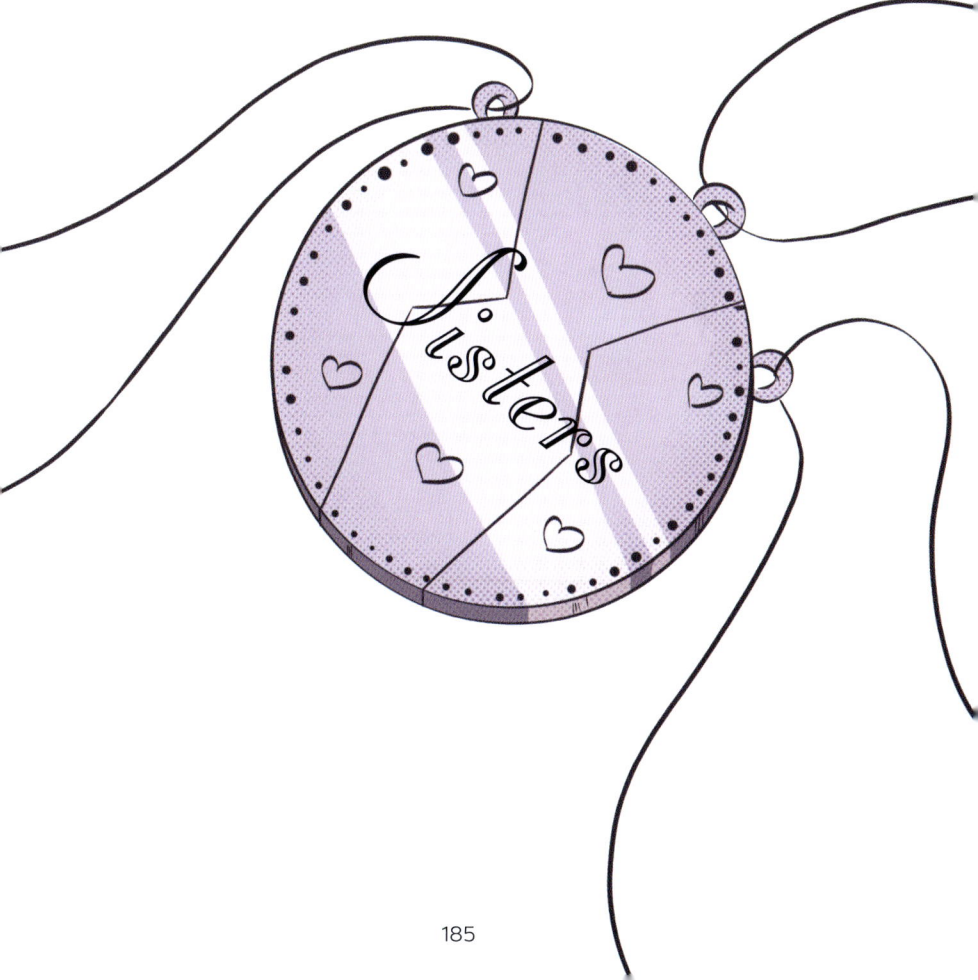

Epilogue

AKA MORE STUFF YOU SHOULD KNOW

ACKNOWLEDGMENTS

THANKS TO:

Matthew Federman, for being an amazing partner and sounding board. And to my son, Fletcher, for putting up with the long hours I spent drawing.

My little brother, Corey Waterman, for being the Devon to my Kennedy.

My editor, Alyson Heller. This book would not exist without you, and it wouldn't be half as fun! You find the impossible solutions that make everyone happy.

My art director, Laura Lyn DiSiena, who encouraged me to push my artwork in countless ways.

My talented team at Aladdin: Valerie Garfield, Kristin Gilson, Anna Jarzab, Christina Solazzo, Sara Berko, and Kilson Roque, who helped shape this book and get it to the right readers.

My marvelous agent, Jennifer March-Soloway, who offered me representation after reading an early version of this book. You connected with my foolishness and said, "Yes, please!" I don't know how I got so lucky.

Jennie Palmer, Greg Pincus, and Matthew Rivera, for your invaluable input along the way.

And to the readers: I hope *Story Spinners* is your new FSF (favorite-story-forever).

CASSANDRA FEDERMAN

has been many things—a hand model, a wrestler, a manatee rescuer, an actor, and a mystic wood elf—but her favorite so far has been an author-illustrator. Her previous books include *This Is a Sea Cow* and *This Is a Seahorse*, which won an International Literacy Association (ILA) Children's & Young Adults' Book Award. *Story Spinners* is her debut middle-grade graphic novel. Visit her online at CassandraFederman.com.